A Winter Walk

A Winter Walk

by LYNNE BARASCH

TICKNOR & FIELDS · New York · 1993

Ticknor & Fields
A Houghton Mifflin company,
215 Park Avenue South, New York, New York 10003.

Manufactured in the United States of America
The text of this book is set in 18 point Usherwood Medium.
The illustrations are watercolor paintings, reproduced in full color.
Book design by Mina Greenstein

HOR 10 9 8 7 6 5 4 3 2 1

Library of Congress Cataloging-in-Publication Data

Barasch, Lynne.
     A winter walk / by Lynne Barasch.
          p.   cm.
     Summary: Sophie and her mother go out in search of the colors of
winter.
     ISBN 0-395-65937-X
     [1. Winter—Fiction.   2. Color—Fiction.]   I. Title.
PZ7.B22965Wi   1993
[E]—dc20   92-39804   CIP   AC

For Ken

ONE cold, gray day, Sophie looks out the window. She feels cold and gray too.

"Let's go for a walk," Mom says, "and we'll
    find the color of winter."
"What color?" says Sophie, but she puts on her
    warm clothes and goes anyway.

Sophie sees a cold, gray world until Mom
picks a bunch of berries,

and the color of winter is red.

Sophie walks through the fields.

The color of winter is rust . . . and yellow,

green . . . and brown,

lavender...and gold.

All these are the color of winter.

Sophie hears a distant sound.

The color of winter is blue.

Something moves. Sophie looks into a pair of brown eyes.

She reaches out,

but the rabbit runs away.

The day turns colder,

and Sophie looks for her Mom.

Snow is falling.

Now the color of winter is white.